ICE AGE™

Popcorn
ELT
Readers

Meet ...
everyone from ICE AGE

It is the start of the ice age.
There is ice in the mountains.
It is cold and everyone is
hungry ...

I'm **Sid**. I'm
a sloth.

I'm **Diego**. I'm a
sabre-toothed tiger.

Sid

Diego

New Words

fall

The cat is **falling**.

camp

They live in a **camp**.

fight

The boys are **fighting**.

disappear

And now the boy **disappears**!

find

I can't **find** my shoe!

help

The boy is **helping** his mother.

hurt

My foot is **hurt**.

ice

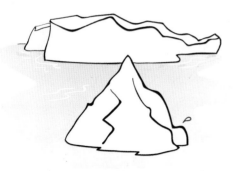

The **ice** is very cold.

mountains

These **mountains** are very big.

volcano

A **volcano** is very hot.

'Yippee!'

Yippee!

What is an ice age? Ask your teacher.

CHAPTER 1
The baby

'Oh no!' shouts Sid the sloth. Some big
animals are running after him.

Manny the mammoth helps him.

'Thank you,' Sid says. 'Do you want a friend?'

Manny does not want a friend.
'Go away!' he says.
But Sid does not go away.

Diego is a tiger. He lives with his friends in the mountains. They are hungry.

One day, they see some men and women in a camp. They have a baby.

'We can eat the baby,' Diego says.

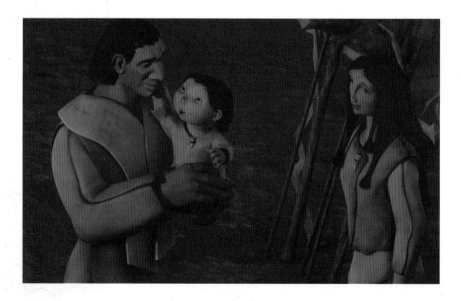

In the morning, the tigers go to the camp. Diego runs after the woman and her baby.

The woman sees Diego. She runs into the water with the baby. But Diego does not like water.

Sid and Manny are walking.

'Look!' Sid says. 'There's a woman with a baby in the water.'

They help the baby. But the mother falls into the water and disappears.

'It's our baby now,' says Sid, but Manny is not happy.

'No, Sid,' says Manny. 'Let's look for his dad.'

'But where can we find him?' Sid asks.

CHAPTER 2
Good friends

Suddenly Manny and Sid see Diego.
  'Give that baby to me,' Diego says.
  'No! We're looking for his dad,' says Manny.

'I can help you,' Diego says. 'The men and women live in a camp in the mountains. Come with me!'

'OK, let's go,' says Manny.

But Diego is not going to the camp. He is going to the tigers.

At night, the animals are tired, but Diego does not sleep. He wants the baby, but Manny has the baby. Diego is angry.

That night, Diego goes to his friends.
'Where's the baby?' they ask.
'He's with the mammoth and the sloth,'
Diego says.
'Good!' the tigers say. 'We can eat the
mammoth and the sloth too!'

In the morning, Diego walks up the
mountain with Sid and Manny. Up and up
they go. Then they go down the ice.

'Yippee!' shouts Diego. Diego and Sid
laugh. They are friends now.

The animals find a volcano. Suddenly Diego falls. Manny helps him.

'Thank you, Manny!' Diego says.

Manny and Diego are good friends now.

The animals are happy. They love the baby and they play with him.

One day, the baby walks. He walks to Diego. Diego and the baby are friends now.

CHAPTER 3
'Goodbye, baby!'

The tigers find Diego with his friends and the baby.

'Hey, Diego!' they shout. 'We're hungry!'

But Diego does not help the tigers.

'Go away!' Diego says. 'These animals are my friends.'

The tigers are very angry. They fight Diego and Manny.

Diego is hurt. He can't walk.
'Go and find the baby's dad,' he says.
'Goodbye, my friends.'
Sid and Manny are very sad.

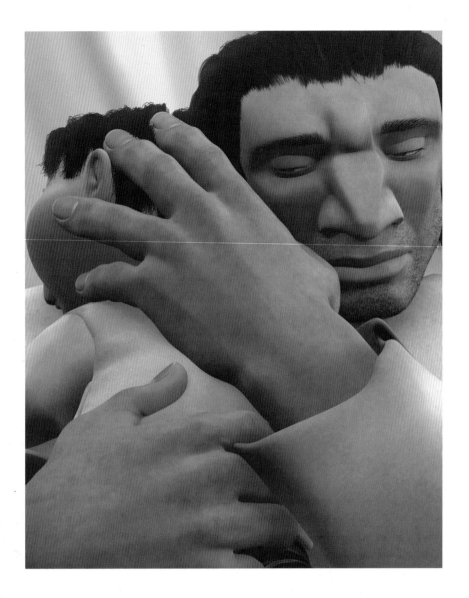

Manny and Sid find the men and women.
The dad sees his baby and he is very happy.
He looks at Manny.

'Thank you!' he says.

The men and women go home.

'Goodbye, baby,' Sid says.

Manny and Sid are very sad again.

'Now there's no baby and no Diego,' Sid says.

Suddenly they see Diego.

'Hello, my friends!' he says.

'Diego! Are you OK?' Sid asks.

'Yes,' Diego says. 'I can walk with you again.'

'A mammoth, a tiger and a sloth!' Sid says.
'We're funny friends, but we're happy!'

THE END

Real World

ICE AND SNOW

In an ice age, it is very cold for many years. There is no summer. We are not in an ice age now. But in some countries it is very cold in winter.

Lapland

Lapland is in the Arctic Circle.

Did you know ...?

In Lapland ...

❄ There are six months of winter.

❄ In winter it is very dark all day. It can be -30°C.

❄ In summer it is not dark at night. It is sunny at twelve o'clock at night!

❄ What time is it dark in your country in winter? And in summer?

reindeer

Reindeer

There are a lot of reindeer in Lapland. Reindeer have a lot of hair. They are not cold in winter.

❄ What animals can you see in the winter in your country?

Fun in the snow

People live in Lapland too. The children have fun in the snow. They play on sledges.

❄ What do you do in the winter in your country?

sledge

What do these words mean? Find out.
snow   summer   winter   months   fun

After you read

1 Circle the right words.

a) Manny and Sid find a **baby** / **sloth**.

b) Sid and Manny look for the baby's **mum** / **dad**.

c) At the start of the story, Diego is **good** / **bad**.

d) Diego falls into **the water** / **a volcano**.

e) Manny **helps** / **does not help** Diego.

f) Manny and Sid give the baby to the **tigers** / **men and women**.

g) At the end of the story, Diego is friends with **Manny and Sid** / **the tigers**.

2 Make sentences. Read and match.

a) Manny and Sid

b) Diego

c) The baby's mum

d) The tigers

e) The baby's dad

i) fights the tigers.

ii) find the baby in the water.

iii) sees the baby and is very happy.

iv) runs into the water with the baby.

v) want the baby.

Where's the popcorn?
Look in your book.
Can you find it?

Puzzle time!

1 Complete the crossword. What words are in the red box?

1. MOUNTAINS
2. cold
3. women
4. baby
5. angry
6. friends

2 Read and count. How many legs?

a) A mammoth, a sloth and a man = ten legs

b) Five men and two tigers = 18

c) Two men, a baby and three women = 12

d) Four mammoths and a cat = 20

e) A mum, a dad, a baby, a dog and a tiger = 14

3 True (✓) or False (✗)? Write in the box.

a) I can see a sloth. ✓

b) There's a woman in the water. ✓

c) There are three mountains. ✓

d) There are two small mammoths. ☐

e) It's a rainy day. ☐

4 Draw your favourite character from the book. Then write a sentence.

This is ...Sid............ .

I like this character

because ...he li is......

......So furry and kind

....

....

....

....

Imagine...

1 Work in groups. Choose one of these scenes from the story.

2 Mime or act the scene. Your friends guess who you are and what you are doing.

You are helping Diego!

You are Manny!

Chant

1 🎧 **Listen and read.**

The start of the ice age
It's the start of the ice age.
There's a lot of ice and snow.
Sid and Manny find a baby
In the ice and snow.

It's the start of the ice age.
There's a lot of snow and ice.
Diego wants the baby
In the snow and ice.

It's the start of the ice age,
And the mountains are big.
There are three friends now
In the mountains so big.

2 🎧 **Say the chant.**